big & SMALL

Original Korean text by Ye-shil Kim
Illustrations by Pauline Comis
Korean edition © Yeowon Media

This English edition published by big & SMALL in 2016
by arrangement with Yeowon Media
English text edited by Joy Cowley
English edition © big & SMALL 2016

Distributed in the United States and Canada by
Lerner Publishing Group, Inc.
241 First Avenue North
Minneapolis, MN 55401 U.S.A.
www.lernerbooks.com

ISBN: 978-1-925248-89-0
Printed in Korea

Hello

Written by Ye-shil Kim

Illustrated by Pauline Comis

Edited by Joy Cowley

The sun greets the butterfly.
Hello, Butterfly!

The butterfly goes
flap, flap, flap
and flies away.

7

The butterfly greets the bee.
Hello, Bee!

The bee goes
buzz, buzz, buzz
and flies away.

The bee greets the rabbit.
Hello, Rabbit!

The rabbit goes
hop, hop, hop
across the grass.

11

The rabbit greets the frog.

Hello, Frog!

The frog goes
croak, croak, croak
on the pond.

The frog greets the duck.

Hello, Duck!

The duck goes
quack, quack, quack
to the farm.

The duck greets the hen.

Hello, Hen!

The hen goes
cluck, cluck, cluck
and waddles away.

The hen greets the lamb.
Hello, Lamb!

The lamb goes
baa, baa, baa
and runs to the pig.

The lamb greets the pig.

Hello, Pig!

But the pig is asleep.

20

21

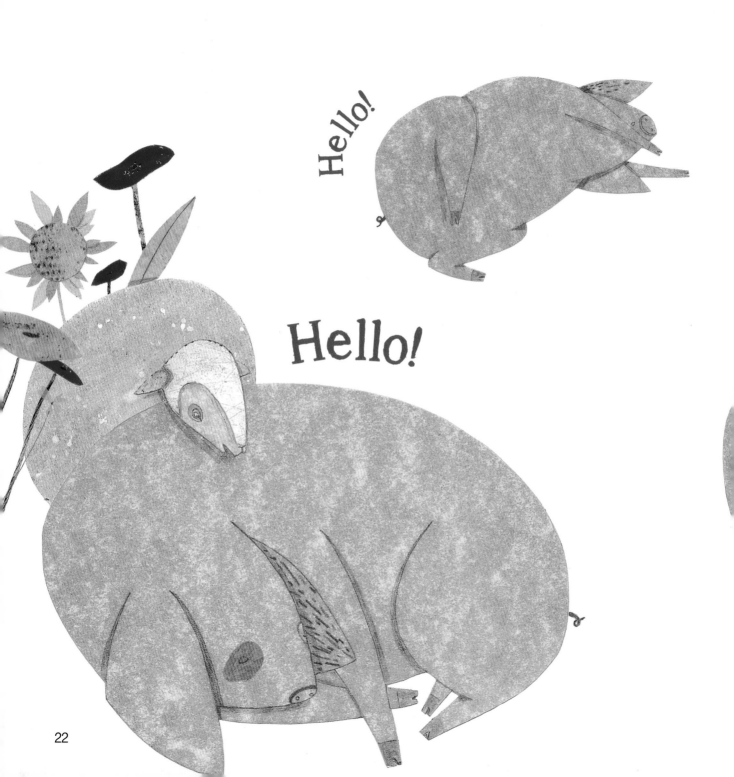

22

Hello!

Hello!

The pig does not wake up.

Lamb calls the others.

They all shout.
Hello, Pig!

26

"I am awake," says the pig.